R.L.   3.9   2pts.

E LEI

2035459

An Ellis Island Christmas

An Ellis Island Christmas

By Maxinne Rhea Leighton · Illustrated by Dennis Nolan

Puffin Books

The art was prepared with watercolor on Bristol paper.

PUFFIN BOOKS
Published by the Penguin Group
Penguin Books USA Inc., 375 Hudson Street, New York, New York 10014, U.S.A.
Penguin Books Ltd, 27 Wrights Lane, London W8 5TZ, England
Penguin Books Australia Ltd, Ringwood, Victoria, Australia
Penguin Books Canada Ltd, 10 Alcorn Avenue, Toronto, Ontario, Canada M4V 3B2
Penguin Books (N.Z.) Ltd, 182-190 Wairau Road, Auckland 10, New Zealand

Penguin Books Ltd, Registered Offices: Harmondsworth, Middlesex, England

First published in the United States of America by Viking Penguin,
a division of Penguin Books USA Inc., 1992
Published in Puffin Books, 1994

9 10

THE LIBRARY OF CONGRESS HAS CATALOGED THE VIKING EDITION AS FOLLOWS:
Leighton, Maxinne Rhea.
An Ellis Island Christmas / by Maxinne Rhea Leighton; illustrated by Dennis Nolan. p. cm.
Summary: Having left Poland and braved ocean storms to join
her father in America, Krysia arrives at Ellis Island on Christmas Eve.
ISBN 0-670-83182-4
[1. Emigration and immigration—Fiction. 2. Polish Americans—Fiction.
3. Christmas—Fiction.] I. Nolan, Dennis, ill. II. Title.
PZ7.L5343El   1992   [E]—dc20 91-47731   CIP   AC

Puffin Books ISBN 0-14-055344-4

Printed in the United States of America
Set in Meridien

To my grandmother Peschka, who inspired this book;
to my friends and colleagues who have held my hand along the way;
and to the reader—may your journey lead you to your own freedom.
—M.R.L.

To George and Rebecca, third generation,
and Erica, fourth generation.
—D.N.

When I was six, my family left Poland to set sail for America.

My mama brought me and my two older brothers, Tomek and Josef, together by the fire. She lit two candles and sang a song to the angels. It was the same song she sang the night Papa left home to go to America.

"I miss my papa," I said.

Mama hugged me. She told us we were going on an adventure. To a new world.

"Papa has found us a beautiful house with trees and flowers in the yard," she said. "In America, tables are filled with food, and there are no soldiers with guns on the street."

Her story sounded like a fairy tale. Most of the time we had food, but sometimes we were hungry, and every street in our village was filled with soldiers. I could not imagine this place called America.

I wanted to see my papa, but I did not want to leave my home and my friend Michi.

That night we packed. We each used the sheets from our beds to wrap our clothes, shoes, a blanket, one toy, and one reading book from school. I had two dolls, but Mama said we had room for only one. Only one! I loved them both, but I took Basha because she was littler than Yola.

Mama tied the four corners of each sheet into a knot for us. We took our big square wicker basket and filled it with some black bread and goat cheese to eat on our journey.

When Mama fell asleep, I crept out of bed with Tomek and Josef. We went near the brook and played in the snow. My brothers built a snowman. I watched the bunnies run away as the stars came into the sky. I made a wish that we would be with Papa again soon.

I said good-bye to my bed, my toys, and to our snowman. I gave my doll Yola a big kiss and told her I'd write to her from America just like Papa wrote to me. I cried. Tomek lifted me in his arms. Josef and Mama put the bundles on their backs. We kissed the door, waved good-bye, and went away. Mama was crying. Tomek, too. My heart felt sad. Josef said we would never see this house again.

It was cold and snowing as we walked through our village. I heard voices call out to us:

"God be with you."

"Until we meet again, dear friends."

"Good luck in America, Petrowskis."

We walked for days through other towns and villages on the way to the sea. My feet hurt from walking and my head hurt from thinking.

"Mama, are we there yet? Are we far from America?"

"Krysia, we have a long way to travel. First we must get to the ship."

I was hungry. Mama said I could not have any more black bread till we got on the boat.

Straight ahead I could see it. A big steamship, waiting to take us to America. We walked very slowly, squashed tight among all the people. As I looked around, I saw no houses, no trees, no animals. Nothing but water and the boat that would take us to Papa.

"Mama, is Papa waiting for us on the boat?"

"No, first we must cross the ocean to get to Ellis Island in America. That's where Papa is waiting for us."

People pushed as we walked up a steep plank of wood to get to the boat. Josef pulled papers out of his pocket with our names and pictures on them. He called them passports. The men in uniform looked at them. They gave us each a number so we'd know which bed to sleep in, and a tin plate with a knife, fork, and spoon.

The beds were close together. One on top of the other. The mattress was like the straw our cows ate. There was no pillow. Mama and I slept in one bed. Tomek and Josef slept in another. It was very cold. Mama wrapped me in her coat to keep me warm. Is this what America was like? I did not know, so I wanted to go home. I missed my warm bed, but most of all I missed Yola.

In the morning, a bell rang for breakfast. The food was not like Mama's. The soup was cold and salty and the bread was white, dry, and hard. I did not like it, but I was hungry, so I ate it all. I heard a girl talking. Then I saw her. It was Zanya! My friend from school.

"Mama, Mama, look! It's Zanya. She's going to America, too!"

Some days it rained and the up-and-down of the bouncy boat made me sick. Mama would put my head in her lap and sing me my favorite song about the angels. It sounded so pretty that when she sang, other people on the boat would sit next to her and sing, too. Then I wasn't sick anymore. I would fall asleep and dream about a nice warm place called home.

By the tenth day of the trip, everyone was throwing up. It was disgusting. It smelled so bad. The water was getting rougher. One afternoon, the sky got black and thick like mud. The ocean got fatter. The waves grew taller and taller as the boat rocked from side to side. Water began to flood the deck.

"Everyone down to your bunks!" the sailors yelled as they pushed us below the deck.

"It's dark down here!" a little boy cried.

We stayed downstairs in our bunk for two days. Every time I stood up, I fell down. We didn't eat or sleep. Maybe we would never reach America.

At the end of the next night, it got very quiet. The boat stopped swaying. From our little window, I could see some purple and blue light in the sky. People cheered when the sailors opened the door to the deck. The cold, salty air danced down the metal stairs into our faces. The sun was just beginning to peek out of the sky. We climbed onto the deck. Dolphins leapt out of the water. The sun was shining and the water was our friend again.

During the day, the men played cards, the women sewed. I played marbles with Zanya. Sometimes I'd bring my doll Basha and she'd bring her doll Ela and we would play house. I'd pretend that we lived in the same town in America in a big house with a peach tree outside.

Zanya's papa was in America, too. Maybe my papa and her papa were best friends like us.

On the fourteenth day, I saw a seagull in the sky. I heard the grown-ups say we were coming closer to America. They were nervous. I was, too. Would they let me into America? Would Papa be there? What would the food taste like?

We could do nothing but wait.

It was the day before Christmas when we did reach America. The sun was shining brightly. Zanya and I were playing dolls. We heard a whistle blow.

Mama ran and pulled us to the deck. She pointed and said, "Look! Look! It's the Lady. The Statue of Liberty. We're in America. America!"

The Lady. She was big. The Lady and so many tall houses, not small ones like in Poland. I felt so little. I closed my eyes and saw the Lady

pick me up and hold me right in the palm of her hand. I could see America better now. Many people. Many faces. Many songs.

The people began pushing as the ship came to a stop. Men in uniforms took us from the ship to a small ferry boat. I felt the salty air push against my face as the boat moved slowly to the dock. Water was ahead of me, behind me, beside me. Then I saw a red-brick building with lots of windows. It was as big as a palace for a king and queen. Mama said it was called Ellis Island. As we got closer, I saw that the building was on a little piece of land with water all around it. "That's why it's called an island," Mama said, "because it's surrounded by water." I wondered if it would float away.

Men in uniforms took us off the boat, leading us down a long metal plank. A man with a beard was yelling, "Stay in line! Move forward! Take your bundles!"

Josef showed him our papers. Then we walked under something long and dark, like a tunnel, and when we saw the sky again, we walked into a very large sunny room. The room seemed as big as our whole village in Poland and it was filled with people and their bundles. Men in high boots and fur caps; ladies in long dresses holding their children. It was noisy; everyone was talking at the same time.

"Hurry. Hurry up. This way. Stay in line. Stay in line." At one end of the room, there was a staircase going up. A man in a uniform pointed his finger, and up the long staircase we went. I saw a flag. It had red and white stripes, and white stars on blue, just like the night sky in Poland. I counted the stars. There were forty-eight. I wondered if each star had a name.

Tomek and Josef went to a line for boys. Mama stayed with me in the line for girls. She said a doctor would examine me and give me papers in English. Then I could see Papa. It was hot. I started to feel dizzy. What if I fell down? Would they let me stay in America?

The doctor put on his glasses. He looked at my face, hair, neck, and hands. He poked at my eyes.

"Fine. She's fine. Here are your papers," he said.

The doctor pinned a ticket on my coat: Krysia Petrowski—555 Fifth Avenue, Brooklyn, New York. My name. Papa's address.

"Move along, little girl. Next. Next."

I saw a lady crying.

"No, no. I am not going back to Europe. I want to stay in America with my child."

The lady's eyes were red. The man with the beard marked an *E* on her back.

"This *E* is for your eyes," he said. "You are sick and must go to the hospital, or else go back to Poland."

The lady and her baby went away. Maybe America would not like me, either.

A bell rang. A man in white gave me milk. Warm milk and two cookies. I was hungry. So hungry that the man gave me three more cookies. Then I saw Mama rushing toward me. Tomek and Josef, too.

"Krysia, we couldn't find you. We thought you were lost."

They sat down on the bench beside me. I told them about the lady with the *E*.

When I finished my warm milk and looked out the window, it was snowing. Just like in Poland. I was happy that it snowed in America, too.

Josef saw a sign and read it out loud. "Milk—three cents; cookies—ten cents; bananas and oranges—ten cents."

"What are cents?" we all asked. Josef explained that just as Polish money was called rubles, American money was called dollars and cents. "I will take our rubles to a man in uniform and he'll exchange it for American dollars."

When Josef returned, he had milk, cookies, and something called a banana. We had never seen a banana before. It was long and yellow with brown spots. I bit into it. It was not tasty, but hard like rubber.

"You don't eat it like that," I heard the milk-and-cookie man say. "You're eating the skin. The tasty part is the inside." I hit the banana on the floor so that it would crack open. The milk-and-cookie man laughed at me.

"Bananas are not smashed open like peanuts, but peeled." Peeled. I did not understand that, so he showed me how to pull the skin off the banana, then he gave me a piece of what was inside. It was mushy and brown. This was good for cows, not for people, I thought, but I ate it anyway.

It was Christmas Eve. We went to sit by the tree in the Great Hall to wait for Papa. The tree looked like a forest. It was so big. So green. Beautiful. All covered with lights and toys. It was dark outside, but the room was as bright as the day. Above me, three big glass circles hung down from the ceiling. I stared into one of them. My eyes began to blink. I had never seen anything in the night shine so brightly, except in storybooks of kings and queens.

In the middle of the room, I saw Zanya's brother playing the violin. Zanya and her mama were dancing. A chubby man with a big belly, in a long white beard and red suit, was laughing. It was Saint Mikolaj, who had made his journey all the way from Poland to America and it was still Christmas Eve. Reindeer must go faster than boats.

The milk-and-cookie man came up beside me. "Yes, that is Saint Mikolaj," he whispered, "but in America the children call him Santa Claus." Santa Claus? I repeated his name over and over again. His name tickled my tongue.

Then Mama took a Christmas surprise out of the wicker basket. It was my other doll, Yola.

"Yola, Yola! I missed you. Were you in the basket all the time?"

"Yes, Krysia," Mama said. "She was sleeping till we got to America."

"But Mama, you said there was room for one doll. Only one."

"Yes. You could take only one." Mama smiled. "But I took the other."

I gave my mama the biggest kiss. Then I hugged my two dolls, Basha and Yola. I lay down on the floor not far from the tree and Mama covered me with my coat. I fell asleep. I saw my new house. Mama was singing the song about the angels, Tomek and Josef were playing checkers, and I was climbing high on top of a peach tree. But where was my papa? I cried to him. He did not answer. Maybe he was lost. Maybe he went away. Maybe he went to Poland to find me. Voices, scary faces—I tried to wake up.

"Papa, Papa."

I opened my eyes. I felt warm hands around my shoulders.

"Papa, you're not lost. You've come. You've come for us!"

Papa smiled. Then he pointed to some words on the wall.

"*To New York,*" he read. "Good-bye, Ellis Island. We are going home."

About This Book

During America's peak immigration years, 1892–1924, seventy percent of the new arrivals entered through Ellis Island—New York City's point of entry. One third of those immigrants chose to stay in New York, while the remainder traveled to other parts of the United States.

People left their homeland for different reasons. Some left in search of jobs, food, religious and political freedom; others to rejoin family members, marry, or simply in search of a new life in a country that many believed had streets paved with gold. The promise of the future fueled each person's desire and overrode the fear of the unknown.

The journey was often an ordeal. Immigrants took only as much of their belongings as they could carry. Most began with a railroad trip to the nearest major seaport where they boarded a huge steamship that carried as many as two thousand passengers. Seas were often rough, bunks overcrowded, and toilet facilities inadequate.

Upon reaching the New York harbor, steerage-class passengers were transferred from the steamship to a barge that took them to Ellis Island. After disembarking, they walked under a canopy, through the Baggage Room, and up the stairs. In the Registry Room (or Great Hall), each person had to go through a routine inspection and medical examination that lasted between three and five hours. Ellis Island inspectors and doctors could often process more than ten thousand immigrants in twenty-four hours. Passing meant entry into America; failing meant detainment or deportment back to the very country the immigrant had just left. However, eighty percent of the immigrants passed and could leave Ellis Island for their final destination. Those who were detained might be held for days, weeks, or months.

For the majority, Ellis Island marked the beginning of a future filled with hope. Today that future is symbolized by the wealth of America—its cultural, racial, and ethnic diversity.

—M.R.L.